In memory of Neil Zucker—S.M.

To my brother, Tom—L.B.

ISBN 0-439-73767-2

Text copyright © 2005 by Steve Metzger.
Illustrations copyright © 2005 by Laura Bryant.
All rights reserved. Published by Scholastic Inc.
SCHOLASTIC and associated logos are trademarks and/or
registered trademarks of Scholastic Inc.

12 11 10 9 8 7 6 5 4 3   5 6 7 8 9/0

Printed in the U.S.A.
First printing, May 2005

FIVE LITTLE SHARKS SWIMMING IN THE SEA

by Steve Metzger

Illustrated by Laura Bryant

SCHOLASTIC INC.

New York   Toronto   London   Auckland   Sydney

Mexico City   New Delhi   Hong Kong   Buenos Aires

Five little sharks swimming in the sea.

One bumped into a giant manatee.

The mother called the doctor and the doctor said,

"NO MORE SHARKS SWIMMING IN THE SEA!"

Four little sharks splashing by the shore.

One got stuck on the ocean floor.

The mother called the doctor and the doctor said,

"NO MORE SHARKS SPLASHING BY THE SHORE!"

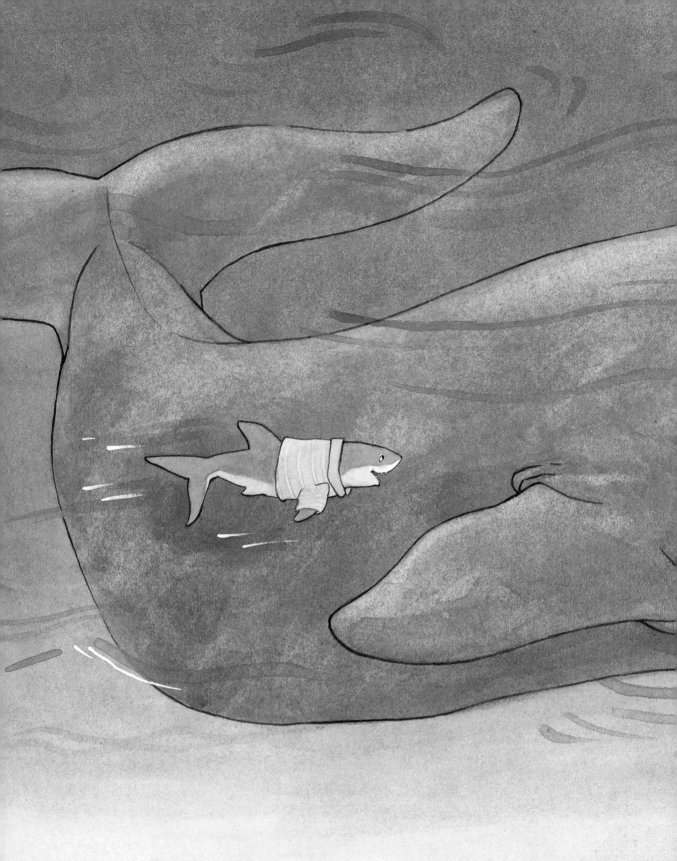

Three little sharks racing past a whale.

One got close and banged his tail.

The mother called the doctor and the doctor said,

"NO MORE SHARKS RACING PAST A WHALE!"

Two little sharks playing hide-and-seek.

One got lost and was missing for a week.

The mother called the doctor and the doctor said,

"NO MORE SHARKS PLAYING HIDE-AND-SEEK!"

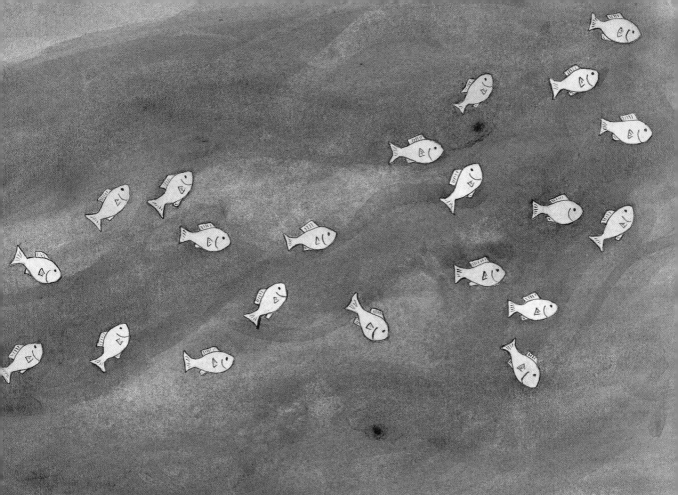

One little shark swimming all alone . . .

. . . ate too many fish and began to groan.

The mother called the doctor and the doctor said,

"NO MORE SHARKS SWIMMING IN THE SEA!"

Now there are . . .
No little sharks swimming in the sea.
No little sharks as happy as can be.

The mother called the doctor and the doctor said,

SWIM WILD AND FREE!"

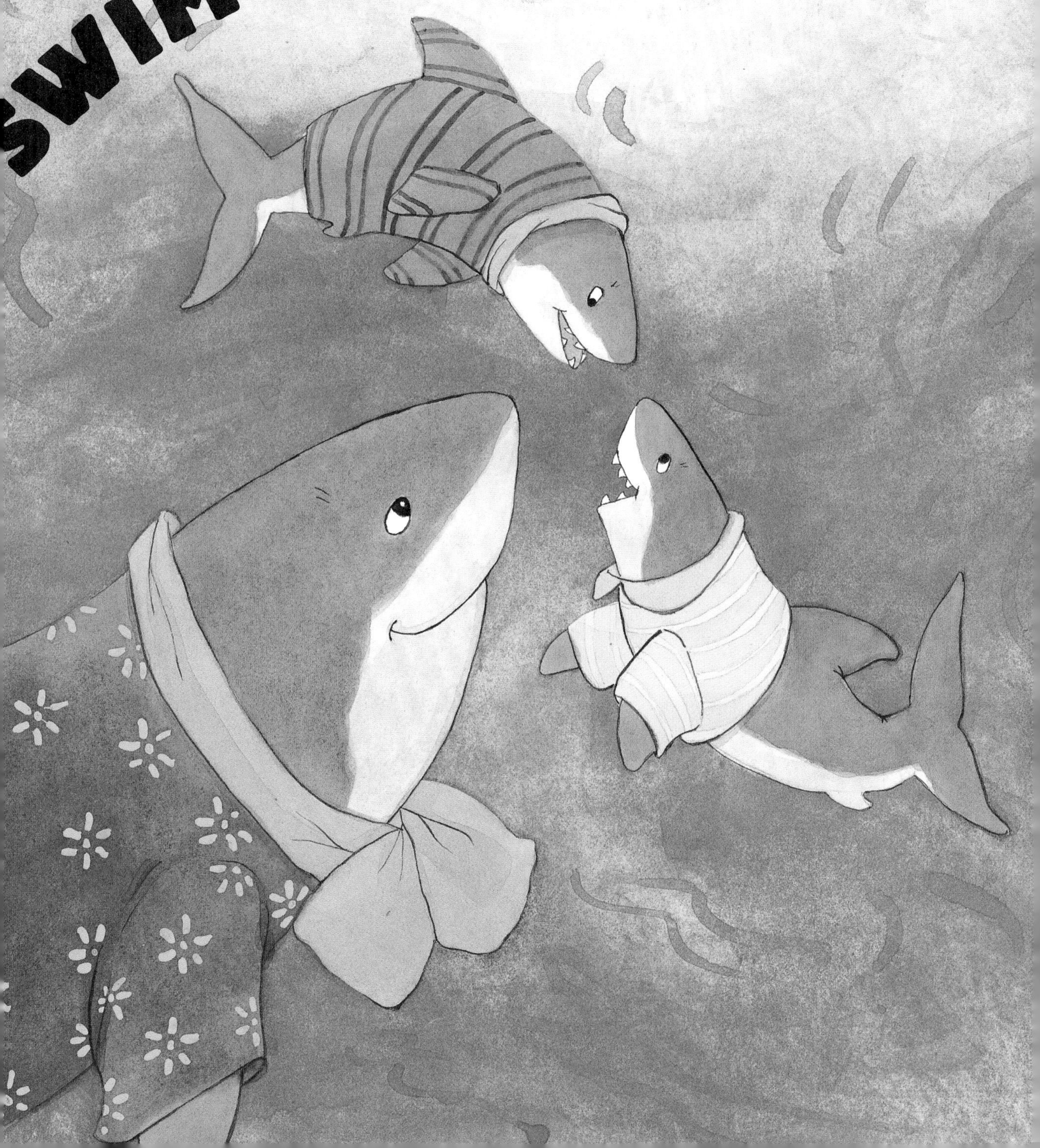